Baby Bigfoot's Journey Home

Written by
Keeley Aramayo

Illustrated by
Miranda Branley

Published by Orange Hat Publishing 2020
ISBN 9781645382539

Copyrighted © 2020 by Keeley Aramayo
All Rights Reserved
Baby Bigfoot's Journey Home
Written by Keeley Aramayo
Illustrated by Miranda Branley

For information, please contact:
Orange Hat Publishing
www.orangehatpublishing.com
Waukesha, WI

To Families of All Shapes and Sizes

In the deep, dark woods lived a baby with big feet.
He had sky-blue eyes, a sweet tooth, and hair that was never neat.

All alone in the dark of night, orphaned Baby
Bigfoot shook with fright.

Gripping his feather pillow tight, Baby Bigfoot
wished for a family with all his might.

Bigfoots were supposed to be modest and stay out of sight.
Baby Bigfoot was different, he needed the spotlight.

So, with a stomp and a clomp, Baby Bigfoot ran from the dark woods into a well-lit neighborhood.

STOMPITY CLOMP! STOMPITY CLOMP! STOMPITY CLOMP!

Before long, Baby Bigfoot needed to rest his feet, so he stopped at the corner bakery for something sweet to eat.

Baby Bigfoot wanted a slice of pie.
The pie was sold out; so, he started to cry.

"Are you alright?" asked a sweet little girl. "You can have my pie, it's cherry with a whipped cream swirl."

The little girl gave Baby Bigfoot her slice of pie and a tissue to dry his drippy, wet eyes.

Without pause, she asked, "Are you all alone? Do you want to come to my home? We can have tea parties, take ballet, and play together every single day. What do you say?"

Baby Bigfoot started to grin,
while cherry pie filling dripped down his chin.

"It's settled then," said the little girl. "My brother you'll be. We will have lots of fun together, you'll see."

Baby Bigfoot smiled because his wish had come true.
His forever family had finally come through!

At home with his sister, Baby Bigfoot enjoyed eating countless tea party treats and playing soccer in his custom-made cleats.

Baby Bigfoot even learned how to grand jeté in his own special way.

At Baby Bigfoot's first ballet recital, he leapt with grace.
He smiled when the warm spotlight shone on his face.

Although the ride home wasn't very far, Baby Bigfoot still fell asleep in the back of the car. Baby Bigfoot's sister rolled him to bed and gave him a great big kiss on the top of his head.

As she turned on Baby Bigfoot's gummy bear nightlight, she heard him whisper...

"I love you, goodnight."

CPSIA information can be obtained
at www.ICGtesting.com
Printed in the USA
LVHW072335271020
670024LV00012B/539